# THE CHURCH'S EMBEZZLEMENT

LYNETTE ALLANA HOPSON

## THE CHURCH'S EMBEZZLEMENT

This incident served as a reminder that even the most respected and trusted individuals can fall prey to greed and corruption. It also highlighted the importance of transparency and accountability in all aspects of life, including religious institutions.

Your life matters to you.

"Let the Life you live speaks for me."

## DEDICATION:

This Book is dedicated to my sons.

Let the life you live speak for you.

Knowing that all that glitters are not gold.

And, that the most respected and trusted

individuals can fall prey to unforeseen.

circumstances.

## TABLE OF CONTENTS

### Chapters

| | |
|---|---|
| 1. The Leader | 7 |
| 2. The Sermon | 10 |
| 3. Embezzlement | 30 |
| 4. Investigation | 36 |
| 5. Confrontation | 41 |
| 6. Shock and Denial | 49 |
| 7. Financial Consequences | 59 |
| 8. Arrest | 64 |
| 9. Healing and Restoration | 68 |
| 10. Conviction | 73 |
| 11. Fall from Grace | 95 |

INTRODUCTION

In the small town of Oakdale, California, Reverend Brown was a respected and beloved preacher at the local church. However, beneath his pious exterior lies a sinister secret: Reverend Brown has been stealing from the church's offering plate to fund his own lavish lifestyle.

Rev. Brown had always been a respected figure in the community. He had led the local church for over a decade, guiding his flock with wisdom and compassion.

However, behind the façade of piety and devotion, Reverend Brown harbored a dark secret. Over the years, he had been embezzling funds from the church. At first, it was a small amount, which he justified as necessary for his own needs. But as time went on, his greed grew, and he began to siphon off larger sums.

Reverend Brown lifestyle began to change. He bought a new car, a luxurious house, and expensive clothes. Deep down, he knew he was living a lie. The truth eventually became known when a diligent church member discovered him pocketing a large amount of money. The congregation was shocked and heartbroken to learn the truth. The church was left to pick up the pieces and rebuild their community.

The incident served as a reminder that even the most respected and trusted individuals can fall prey to greed and corruption. It also highlighted the importance of transparency and accountability in all aspects of life.

Chapter 1

The Leader

The Revered Brown was a man of unwavering integrity and honor, whose very presence commanded respect. For decades, he had been a pillar of strength in his community, spreading +
the message of salvation and hope to all who would listen. Every Sunday, Rev. Brown would stand at the pulpit, his voice booming with conviction as he preached the word of God. His sermons were always filled with passion, compassion, and wisdom, leaving his congregation inspired and uplifted. But Rev. Brown's impact went far beyond the walls of his church. He was a tireless advocate for the poor, the marginalized, and the oppressed. He spent countless hours visiting the sick, the elderly, and the imprisoned,

offering words of comfort and hope. Despite his many responsibilities, Rev. Brown always had time for those in need. He was a listener, a counselor, and a friend to all who sought his guidance. His door was always open, and his heart was always willing to help. As a result, Rev. Brown was deeply loved and respected by his community.

People from all levels of society would come to seek his counsel, his blessing, his prayer, or simply his presence. He was a beacon of hope in a world filled with darkness and despair. Years went by, and Rev. Brown's reputation as a man of God continued to grow. He became a beloved figure in his community, a symbol of faith, hope, and charity. And even as the years draw, his spirit remained strong, his heart remained pure, and his message remained unchanged.

His congregation decided that Rev. Brown's legacy would live on for generations to come, a testament to the power of faith, integrity, and compassion. He could always go down in history as a man of honor, a man of God, and a man who had touched the lives of countless people in profound and lasting ways. His integrity spoke volume to the church. Thus, one of the many reasons why he was chosen to become the Shephard of the community.

Chapter 2

The Sermon

Reverend Brown was seen praying at the church's alter before delivering one of his most powerful sermons to his congregation. He also prayed aloud before he rendered his sermon to his audience.
Rev. Brown's Prayer Rev. Brown stood in the quiet solitude of his congregation, his eyes closed, and his hands clasped together in prayer. He took a deep breath, and his voice, filled with reverence and sincerity, began to pray:
"Dear Heavenly Father, I come before you today, humbled and grateful for the opportunity to serve you and your people. I pray that you will anoint me with your Holy Spirit, that I might preach your word with power, conviction, and compassion. "Lord, I pray

that you will prepare the hearts of your people to receive your message. May they be open to your truth, and may they be transformed by your power. "Give me wisdom, Lord, to speak your words in a way that is both faithful to your scripture and relevant to the needs of your people. May my words be seasoned with salt, and may they bring hope, encouragement, and challenge to all who hears them. "Protect me, Lord, from the temptations of pride, ego, and self-interest. May I remain humble, dependent on you, and focused on your glory. "Finally, Lord, I pray that you will be glorified in all that I do today. May my sermon be a reflection of your love, your mercy, and your grace. May your people be blessed, and may your name be exalted. "In Jesus' name, I pray. Amen." As Rev. Brown finished his prayer,

He felt a sense of peace and confidence wash over him. He knew that he was ready to preach, and that God would be with him every step of the way. As he spoke, the camera focuses throughout the faces of the parishioners, showing their devotion and admiration for their preacher. They were diligently digesting every spoken syllable.

The scripture for the day was taken from Exodus Chapter 20:

The highlights were as follows: Exodus chapter 20, contains the Ten Commandments,

It is also known as the Decalogue. Here is a summary, The Ten Commandments (Exodus 20:1-17) 1. Worship only God (Exodus 20:3) 2. Make no idols (Exodus 20:4-5)

3. Do not take God's name in vain (Exodus 20:7)

4. Remember the Sabbath (Exodus 20:8-11)

5. Honor your parents (Exodus 20:12)

6. Do not murder (Exodus 20:13)

7. Do not commit adultery (Exodus 20:17)

8. Do not steal (Exodus 20:15)

9. Do not bear false witness (Exodus 20:16)

10. Do not covet (Exodus 20:17)

The Ten Commandments serve as a foundation for moral principles and guidelines for living a righteous life. They emphasize the importance of worshiping and honoring God, respecting others, and living with integrity. You may ask, what was the main theme or message of the sermon on

1. Establishing a covenant relationship: God was establishing a covenant relationship with the Israelites, and the Ten Commandments served as the terms of that agreement.

2. Setting moral standards: The Ten Commandments provided a moral framework for the Israelites to live by, distinguishing them from other nations.

3. Defining worship and obedience

Exodus 20 emphasized the importance of worshiping only God and obeying His commands.

4. Providing a basis for justice and righteousness

The Ten Commandments served as a foundation for justice, righteousness, and morality in Israelite society.

5. Preparing the Israelites for the Promised Land

Before entering the Promised Land, God wanted to ensure that the Israelites understood His expectations for their behavior and worship.

6. Revealing God's character and nature

The Ten Commandments reflect God's character, revealing His holiness, justice, and love. By giving the Ten Commandments, God aimed to create a holy and righteous people who would reflect His character and bring glory to Him.

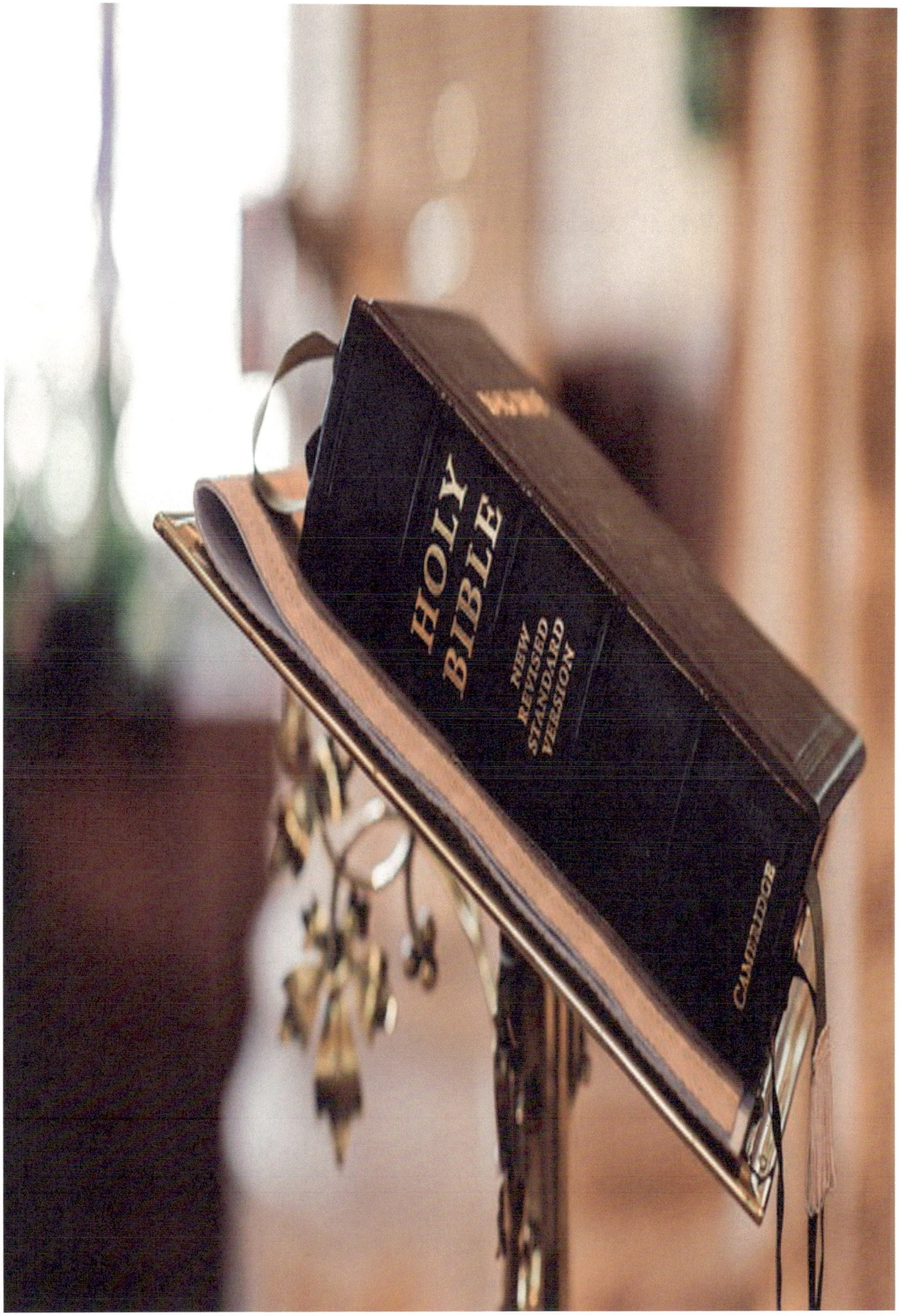
HOLY
BIBLE
NEW
REVISED
STANDARD
VERSION
CAMBRIDGE

Rev. Brown stood at the pulpit, his voice booming through the crowded church. His sermon was on the Ten Commandments, and he spoke with conviction, his eyes scanning the congregation. "Thou shalt not commit adultery," he declared, his voice dripping with righteousness. "Thou shalt not bear false witness. Thou shalt not covet." But when he came to the eighth commandment, "Thou shalt not steal,"

Rev. Brown's tone faltered for a moment. He cleared his throat, his eyes darting nervously around the room.

"Yes, my friends," he continued, his voice recovering its usual strength. "We must respect the property of others. We must not take what is not ours."

Preaching such a sermon and knowing the truth. The truth? Rev. Brown was embezzling church funds. He had been stealing from the church for months, using the money to finance his own lavish lifestyle.

As the sermon ended, Rev. Brown's congregation applauded, inspired by his words. Little did Rev. Brown know that his hypocrisy would eventually be exposed.

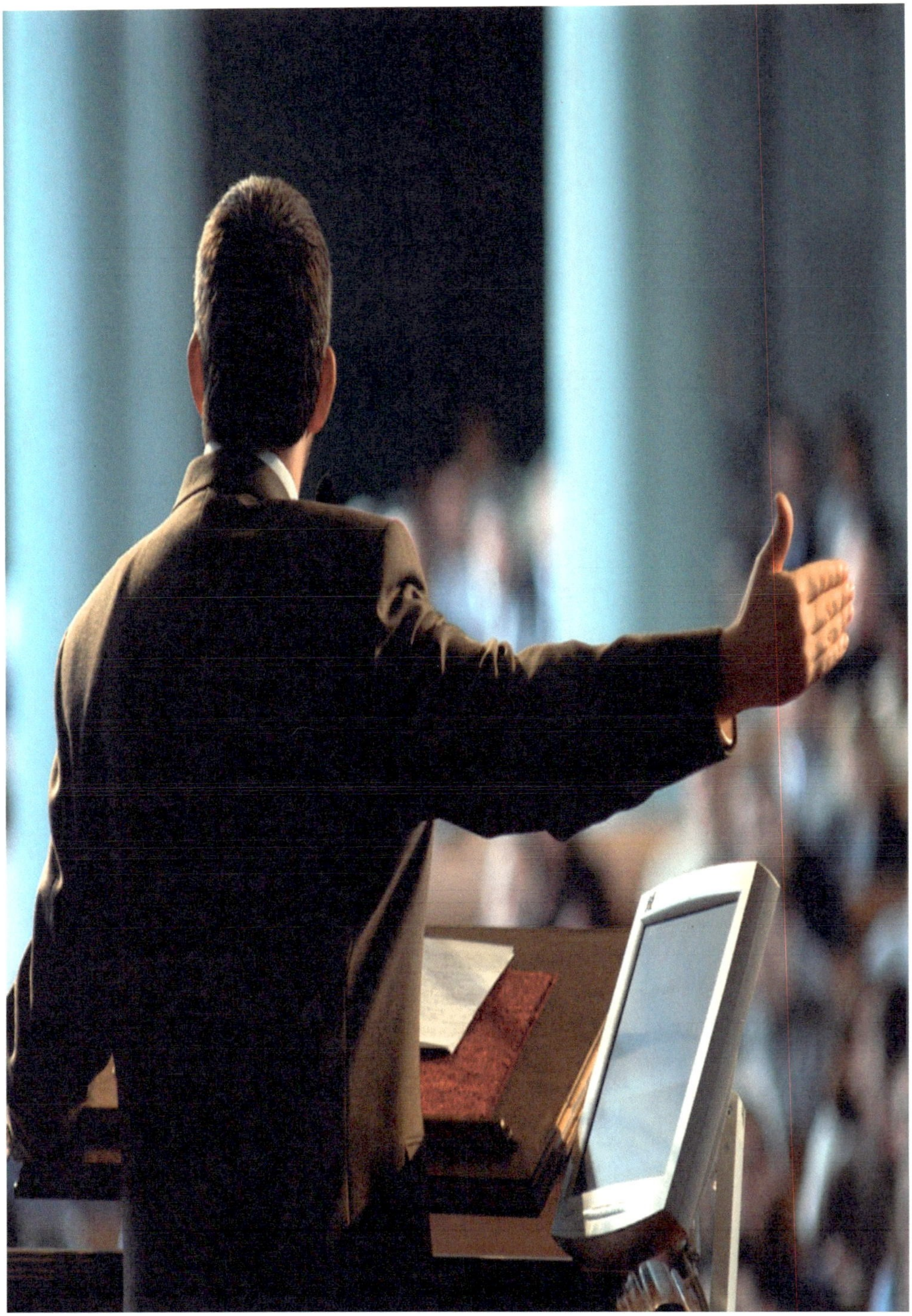

Rev. Brown preached again during the Evening Assembly. As the congregation filed out of the church, they were buzzing with excitement and inspiration from Reverend Brown's powerful sermon on John 3:16. They were elated to have such a fine intelligent person leading them. They love and respect him very much.

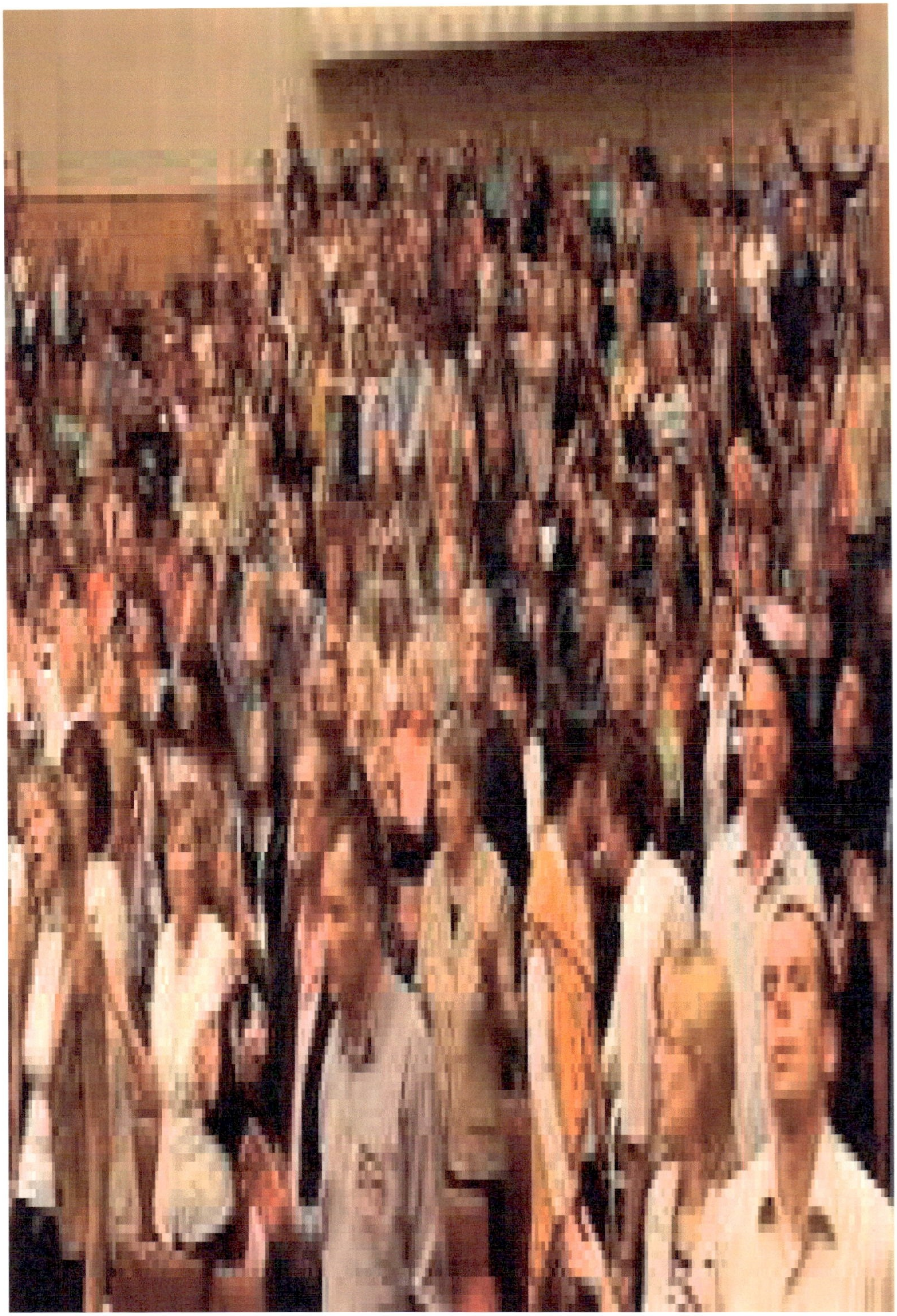

Despite the secret sin he had committed just hours before, Reverend Brown had managed to convey the depth of God's love with conviction and passion. "For God so loved the world that he gave his one and only Son, that whoever believes in him shall not perish but have eternal life." Reverend Brown's voice had rung out across the sanctuary, filling the hearts of his listeners with hope and joy.

As he stood at the door later that evening shaking hands and exchanging warm smiles with his parishioners, Reverend Brown could not shake the feeling of guilt and hypocrisy that gnawed at his soul. Little did he know his deceit would soon be exposed, and his congregation would be left reeling from the deceit.

One week later, Rev. Brown stood before his congregation: "Praise the Lord Church. I have had a tough time choosing a message for today. I had my mind set on numerous books, and chapters of the Bible, However, Proverbs 3:33 kept pulling at my heart. Therefore, I will focus on that book and verse for today. OK, Proverbs 3:33 states: "The Lord's curse is on the house of the wicked, but he blesses the home of the righteous. Let us repeat that once again.

This message is for each one of us.
This verse highlights the contrast between the consequences of wickedness and righteousness. It emphasizes that God's blessing and curse are directly tied to our actions and choices.

In the context of Proverbs 3:33, "wicked" refers to individuals who consistently exhibit evil, immoral, or unethical behavior. The Hebrew word used in this verse, "Rasha," means evil, guilty, offender, ungodly it actually describes someone who: 1. Deliberately violates God's laws and principles.

2. Shows disregard for the well-being and rights of others.

3. Engages in sinful and destructive behaviors. Some common characteristics of wicked individuals include:

1. Dishonesty and Deception

2. Cruelty and lack of compassion

3. Rebellion against authority and God's laws

4. Exploitation and manipulation of others

5. Arrogance and a lack of humility

6. Shun the right engage in the wrong

In contrast, the "righteous" person, as mentioned in Proverbs 3:33, is someone who:

1. Follows God's laws and principles.

2. Shows kindness, compassion, and respect for others.

3. Strives to live a moral and ethical life. The distinction between wicked and righteous individuals is not about perfection but about the overall direction and intent of their lives. Where do you fit in? Which one applies to you? Are you righteous or wicked? You go figure that one out.

Its right here in the Bible, Church. The Lord's curse is on the house of the wicked, but he blesses the home of the righteous. Imagine two homes, side by side, yet worlds apart. One home is filled with the sound of laughter and love, where family members care for one another and live with integrity. They are certain that each need is met. Protection, guidance, and safekeeping are established. This is the home of the righteous.

Next door, a different story unfolds. The home of the wicked is marked by deceit, dishonesty, and disrespect. The mom shoplifts. The dad is junky. The atmosphere is always bouncing with tension; and the air is heavy with the weight of sinful choices. The joy of laughter is missing.

The wife's face is black and blue, children are running to hide when the dad's car enters the driveway. The prayer alter has disappeared from home. The shouting and arguing exist outside the front door. Clearly this could not be the house of a righteous.

The Lord looks down on these two homes, and His response is clear. He curses the house of the wicked, bringing consequences for their sinful ways. But He blesses the home of the righteous, showering them with favor, protection, and joy.

This is not a promise of a trouble-free life, but a guarantee that God's presence and blessing will rest on those who follow Him. The righteous may face challenges, but they will face them with the confidence of God's love and care.

In contrast, the wicked may seem to prosper for a time, but their success is short-lived. Their choices will lead to destruction, and they will face the consequences of their sinful actions.

Church, the choice is clear. Which home will you choose? Will you follow the path of the righteous, or will you succumb to the temptation of wickedness? The Lord's blessing or curse hangs in the balance.

"Church, I urge you to choose righteousness!" May we, as the body of Christ, strive to live lives that reflect God's righteousness. May we choose to: Walk in obedience to God's Word, Love and serve one another, stand for justice and compassion, seek holiness and humility, may our choices bring glory to God and inspire others to follow Him.

As Proverbs 3:33 reminds us: "The Lord's curse is on the house of the wicked, but He blesses the home of the righteous." Let us choose righteousness, church! Amen

Let us pray: "Dear Heavenly Father, we come before you today, grateful for the opportunity to gather as your church. We thank you for the powerful sermon we heard today, focusing on Proverbs 3:33. Lord, we acknowledge that your Word is alive and active, speaking directly to our hearts. We pray that you will bless your church as we focus on the wisdom found in Proverbs 3:33. May we, as your people, take to heart the importance of choosing righteousness. May we strive to live lives that reflect your character, seeking to honor you in all we do. Bless our church, Lord, as we seek to apply the principles found in your Word. May we be people who walk in obedience, love, and humility. May our lives reflect your goodness and glory. We pray for your continued guidance and wisdom. May your Holy Spirit empower us to live out our faith in a way that brings honor to you. In Jesus' name, we pray. Amen

## Chapter 3:

## Embezzlement

After the service, Reverend Brown was seen sneaking into the church office to count the day's offerings. As he tallies up the donations, he cannot resist the temptation to pocket a considerable sum of money.

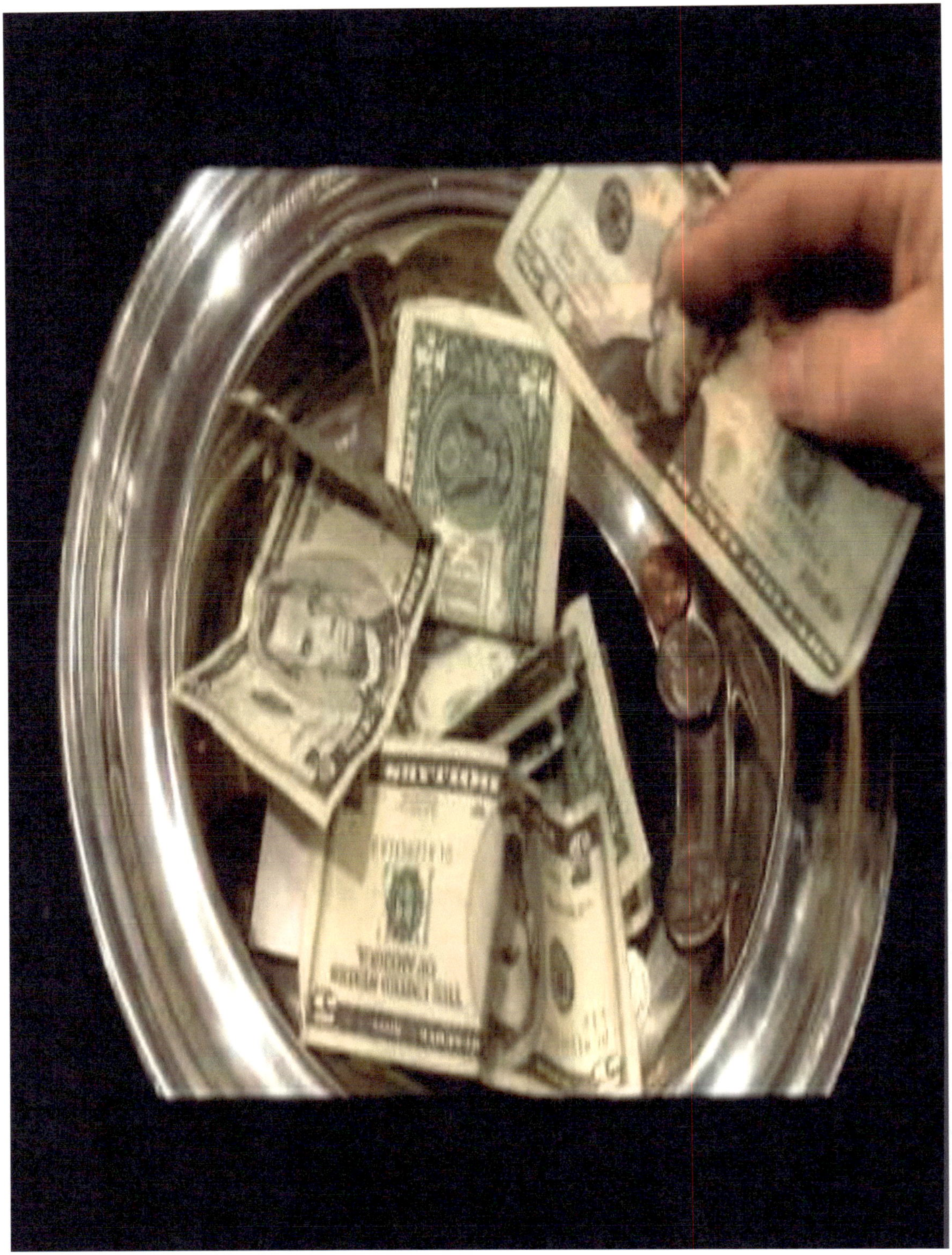

A skilled investigative journalist had recently moved to Oakdale to escape the stress of her high-pressure job in the city. She was drawn to Reverend Brown's charismatic sermons and the sense of community at the church. However, during her third visit to the church, Sarah noticed something that caught her attention.

As she was dropping off her offering envelope, she saw Reverend Brown quickly stuffing a large wad of cash into his pocket. He seemed nervous and furtive, and Sarah's journalist instincts kicked in. She began to wonder if Reverend Brown was misusing church funds. She started attending more services, observing Reverend Brown's behavior, and asking discreet

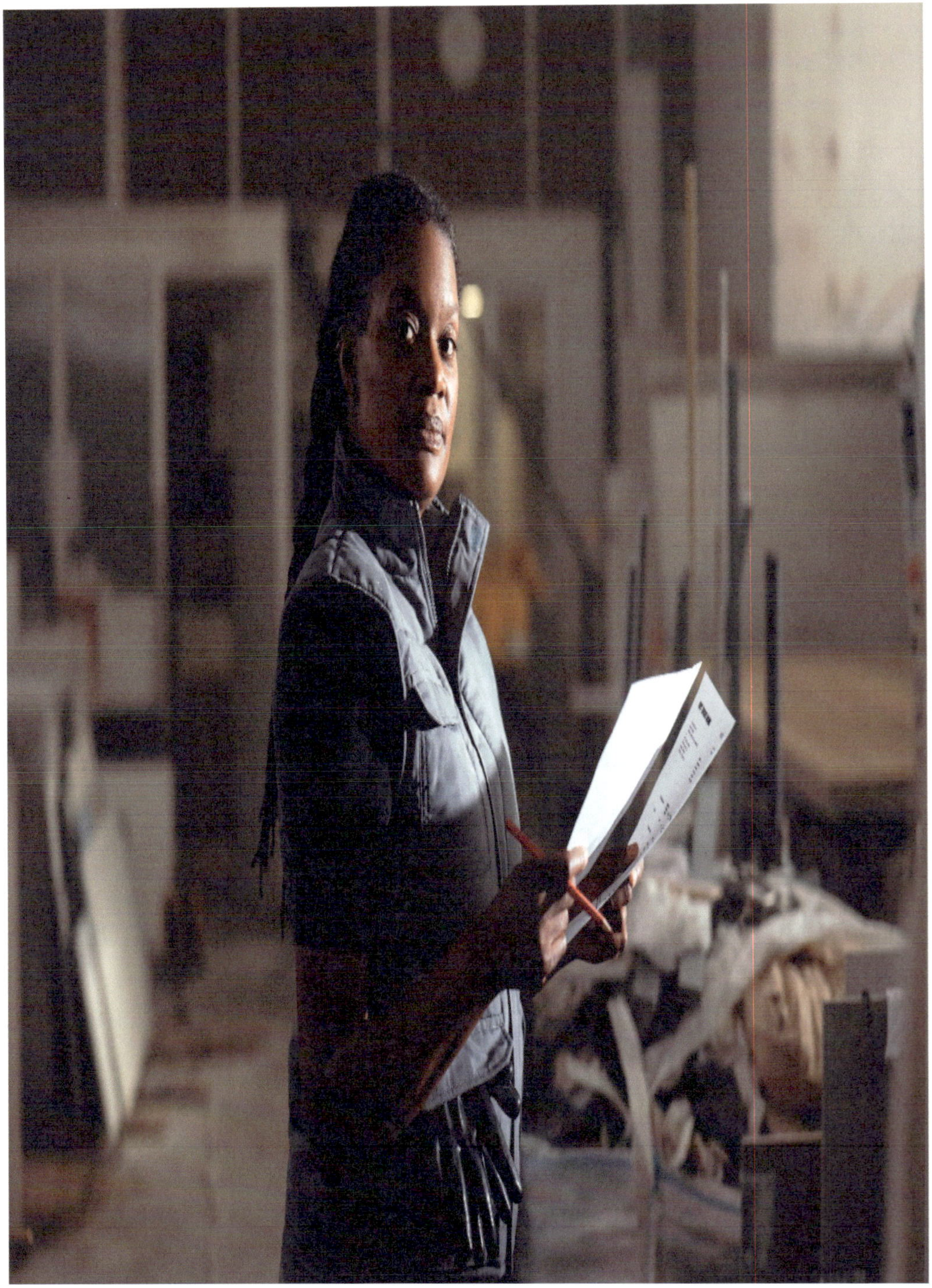

questions to other church members. As she dug deeper, Sarah discovered that Reverend Brown's lifestyle seemed inconsistent with his modest salary as a preacher. He drove a luxury car, wore expensive suits, and frequently took exotic vacations. These red flags sparked Sarah's curiosity, and she decided to investigate further.

Rev. Brown was a respected member of the church community, known for his leadership and guidance. But this suspicious behavior raised questions. As many questions were asked by Sarah, the church council decided to investigate too.

They approach him privately; however, he denied every aspect of their interrogations.

## Chapter 4:

## The Investigation

Meanwhile, Sarah begins to suspect that something is amiss. She starts to investigate Reverend Brown's finances more in depth. She discovers that despite his modest salary, he was living a life of luxury, with expensive cars, lavish vacations, and a grand house. The council members were baffled. "How could he afford all this on our small church's budget?" one of them asked. As they dug deeper, they discovered some suspicious transactions and embezzlement. Rev. Brown might have been using church funds for his own personal gain.

The investigation into Rev. Brown's finances revealed even more shocking secrets. It turned out that he owned a luxurious house in a gated community in another country, complete with a private pool, tennis court, and stunning views. But what was even more astonishing was that Rev. Brown had hired a team of staff to oversee the property and prepare it for his frequent vacations.

The team included a personal chef, a housekeeper, and a groundskeeper. The church council was stunned. "How could he afford all this?" they asked. "And why did he keep it a secret?" As the news spread, the church community was rocked by the revelations. Many felt betrayed by Rev. Brown's hypocrisy and lavish lifestyle, which was funded by the church's donation.

The luxurious villa, named "Serenity Oasis," is nestled among the swaying palm trees of a private estate. As you step through the grand entrance, you are greeted by the warm sunshine and the soothing sound of water features. The villa's exterior boasts sleek, modern architecture with expansive glass windows and sliding doors that seamlessly blend indoors and outdoor living. The perfectly manicured lawn is dotted with tall palm trees, their leaves rustling gently in the breeze. At the heart of the property lies a stunning swimming pool, its clear waters reflecting the sun's rays. The pool area is surrounded by comfortable lounge chairs, umbrellas, and an outdoor kitchen perfect for all fresco dining. Inside, the villa features spacious, airy rooms with lofty ceilings, marble floors, and elegant furnishings. Floor-to-ceiling windows and sliding glass doors provide breathtaking views of the surrounding landscape. The villa's luxurious amenities include:

5 spacious bedrooms with luxurious bathrooms: Gourmet kitchen with high-end appliances and ample counter space - Expensive living areas, including a formal lounge and informal family room - Private movie theater - Fitness center and spa –

Outdoor kitchen and dining area - Private parking and garage. Whether you are seeking a relaxing retreat or an entertaining hub, "Serenity Oasis" offers the ultimate luxurious living experience amidst the tranquil beauty of nature.

As the investigation into Rev. Brown's embezzlement scandal deepened, a surprising twist emerged. Further scrutiny of the financial records revealed that a massive portion of the stolen funds had been diverted to support orphanages in various third-world countries. Rev. Brown had been using the ill-gotten gains to fund humanitarian efforts, providing food, shelter, and education to countless children in need. This latest information added a layer of complexity to the case, raising questions about Rev. Brown's motivation and the morality of his actions. Had he truly been driven by a desire to do good, or was this simply a clever attempt to justify his wrongdoing?

As the congregation and the community struggled to come to terms with this revelation, they were forced to confront the difficult intersection of faith, morality, and the gray areas in between.

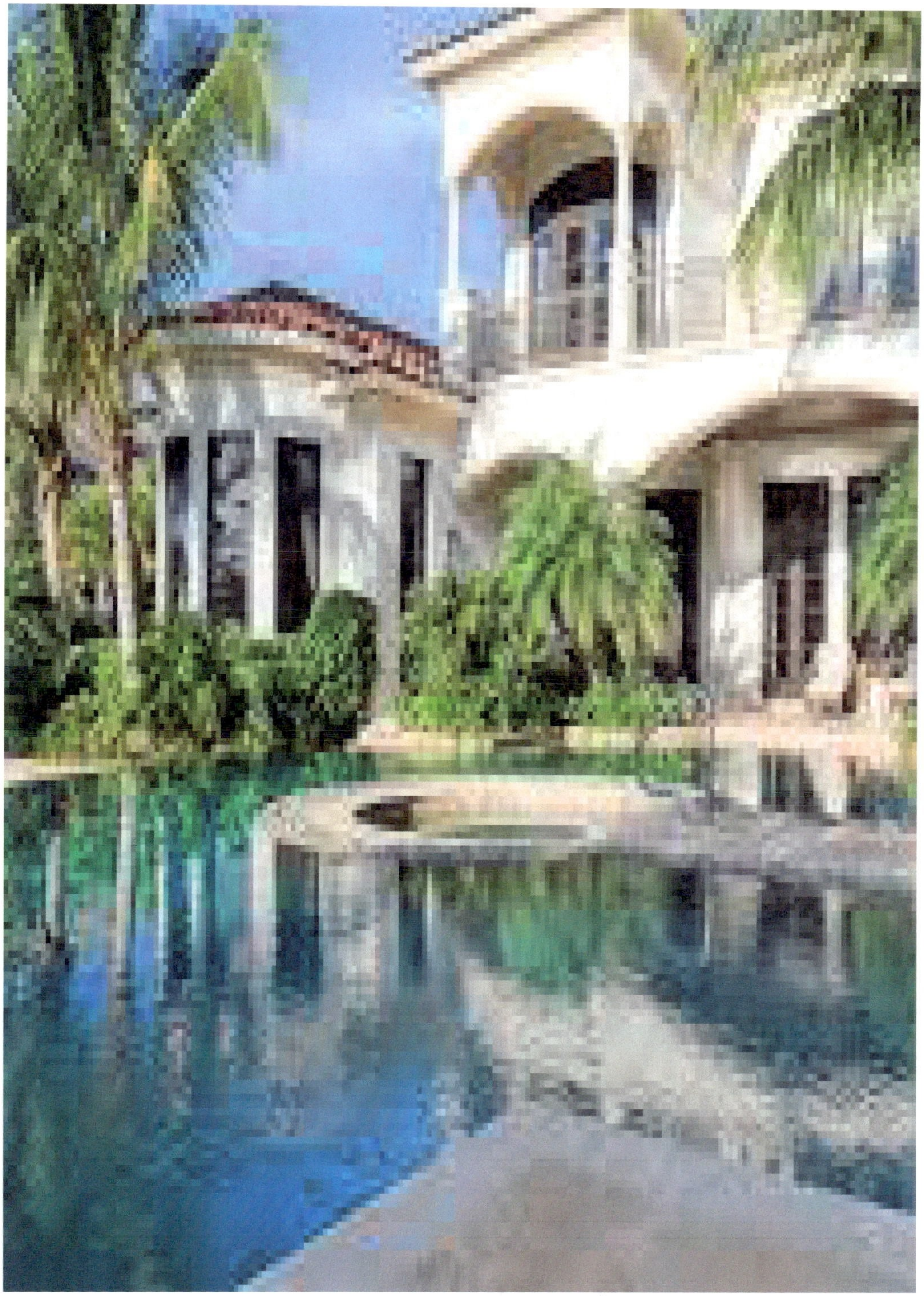

Chapter 5:

Confrontation

As Sarah digs deeper, she confronts Reverend Brown about her findings. The preacher was caught off guard and becomes increasingly defensive and hostile. The church council's investigation had uncovered enough evidence to confront Rev. Brown also. They called him into an emergency meeting, where they shared their findings. Rev. Brown's expression changed from one of confidence to one of shock and guilt. He knew he had been caught. "I....I... can explain," he stammered.

But the council members were unforgiving. "Explain what, Rev. Brown?" one of them asked sternly. What could you have to say to us?

Rev. Brown, No disrespect intended to you as our leader, BUT, NO! YOU LET ME EXPLAIN! "See, what you do not realize is that we appreciated your leadership and service to our church community. We love you as our leader. As we continue to grow and thrive, we kindly encourage our members to consider making sacrifices to support our church's mission and ministries, including providing for your salary. We give you a fruit basket every month. Along with filling your pantry every week. We were grateful to you. We love and appreciate you. For been an outstanding leader in our church. And, therefore, we show it through our actions.

Some of our members are struggling, yet they give diligently so that you will have your weekly salary. And now, to have discovered such defeat. Kindly save your explanation for the judge and juris " This behavior is unacceptable."  You have been stealing from this church and its members?"

Rev. Brown's eyes dropped, and he nodded slowly. "I'm sorry," he whispered.

Reverend Brown was initially defensive and dismissive. However, as the evidence against him mounted, he began to realize the gravity of his situation. "I...I was just borrowing the money," Reverend Brown stammered. "I was going to pay it back, I swore. I've been struggling financially, and I didn't know how else to make ends meet."

When asked about his luxurious lifestyle, Reverend Brown claimed that the car and vacations were gifts from wealthy parishioners who appreciated his ministry. "I didn't want to reveal their generosity publicly, as I didn't want to draw attention away from the Lord's work," Reverend Brown said, attempting to sound devotedly religious.

The congregation's response to Rev. Brown's actions was a mix of shock, disappointment, and understanding. One of the elderly members of the church, Sister Thompson, spoke up, her voice filled with a sense of sadness and regret. "Rev. Brown, we loved and respected you, and we would have gladly supported your efforts to help those in need. You did not have to steal from us to support the orphanage. We would have collected a special contribution for that purpose once a month, or even more often if needed." Sister Thompson's words echoed the sentiments of many in the congregation. They felt that Rev. Brown's actions, although well-intentioned, had been misguided and hurtful. They wondered why he had felt the need to resort to theft, rather than trusting in the generosity and goodwill of the church community. As the congregation grappled with the aftermath of Rev. Brown's actions, they began to realize that his mistakes had also brought to light the church's own potential for compassion and generosity. They saw that they had the power to make a positive impact on the world, and that they did not need to rely on one person's actions to do so.

Sarah produced more devious incriminating documents. The financial records showing that the gifts" were purchases made with church funds, As Reverend Brown's defense began to unravel.

The council members became more outrageous.

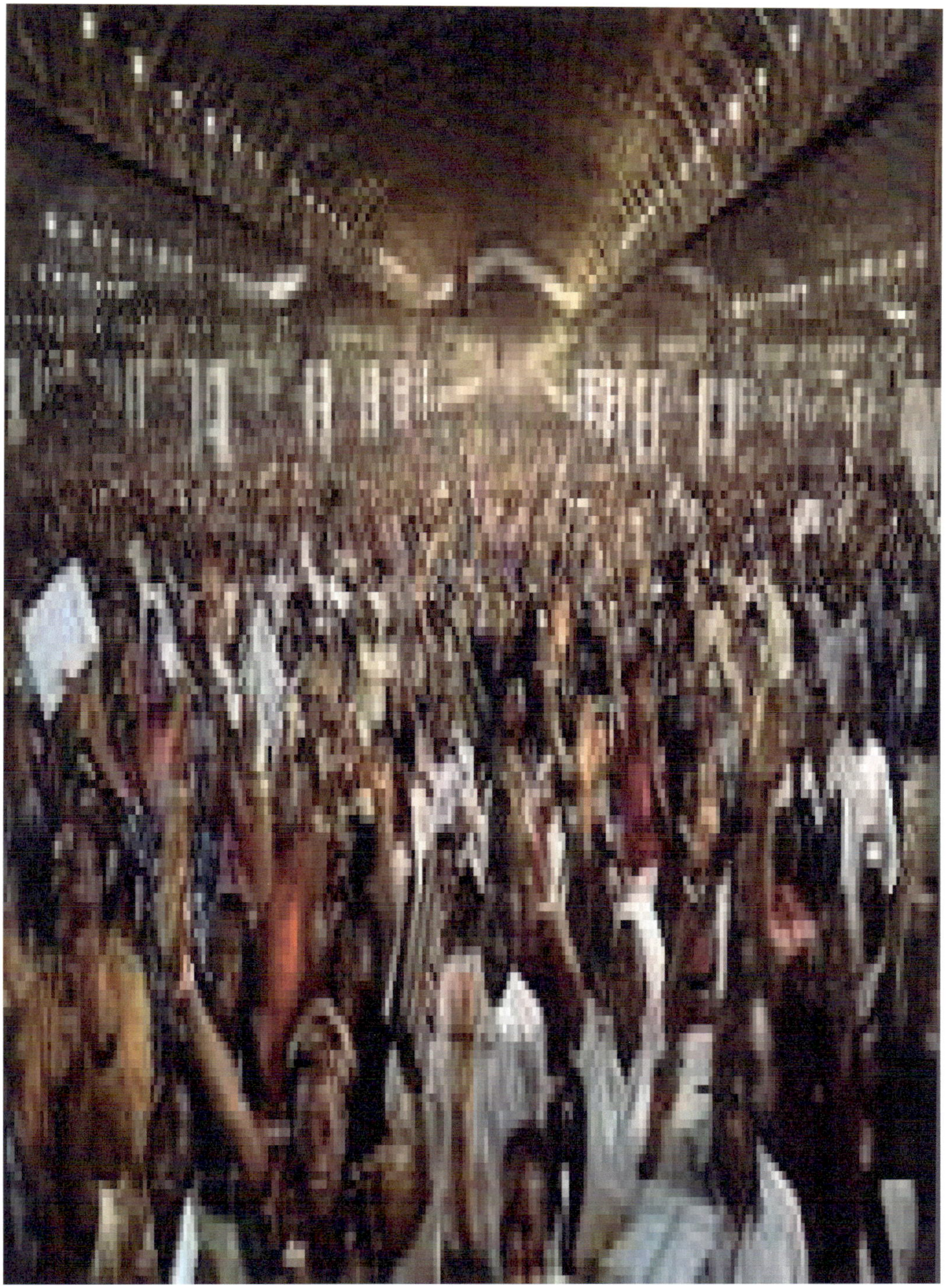

## Chapter 6

Shock and Denial

The news of the deception "spread like while fire . Church members were stunned. They claimed that all were false rumors. My, Reverend Brown's deceitful. No, Many refused to accept the truth, thinking it was a malicious attack on their beloved preacher reputations.

Others were thrown into emotional turmoil, feeling betrayed, angry, and hurt.

Others felt guilty for not recognizing the signs of Reverend Brown's dishonesty sooner.

The church council was forced to take immediate action, suspending Reverend Brown from his duties and launching an investigation into financial irregularities.

The scandal attracted local media attention, with newspapers and TV stations reporting on the story.

This brought unwanted scrutiny to the church and its members.

That is a common reaction in many communities.

Here are some thoughts: The news of Reverend Brown embezzlement sent shockwaves through the church community. As the reality of the situation sank in, church members began to reach out to each other, sharing their thoughts, feelings, and reactions. While some conversations were supportive and focused on praying for the church and its leaders, others quickly turned to gossip and speculation.

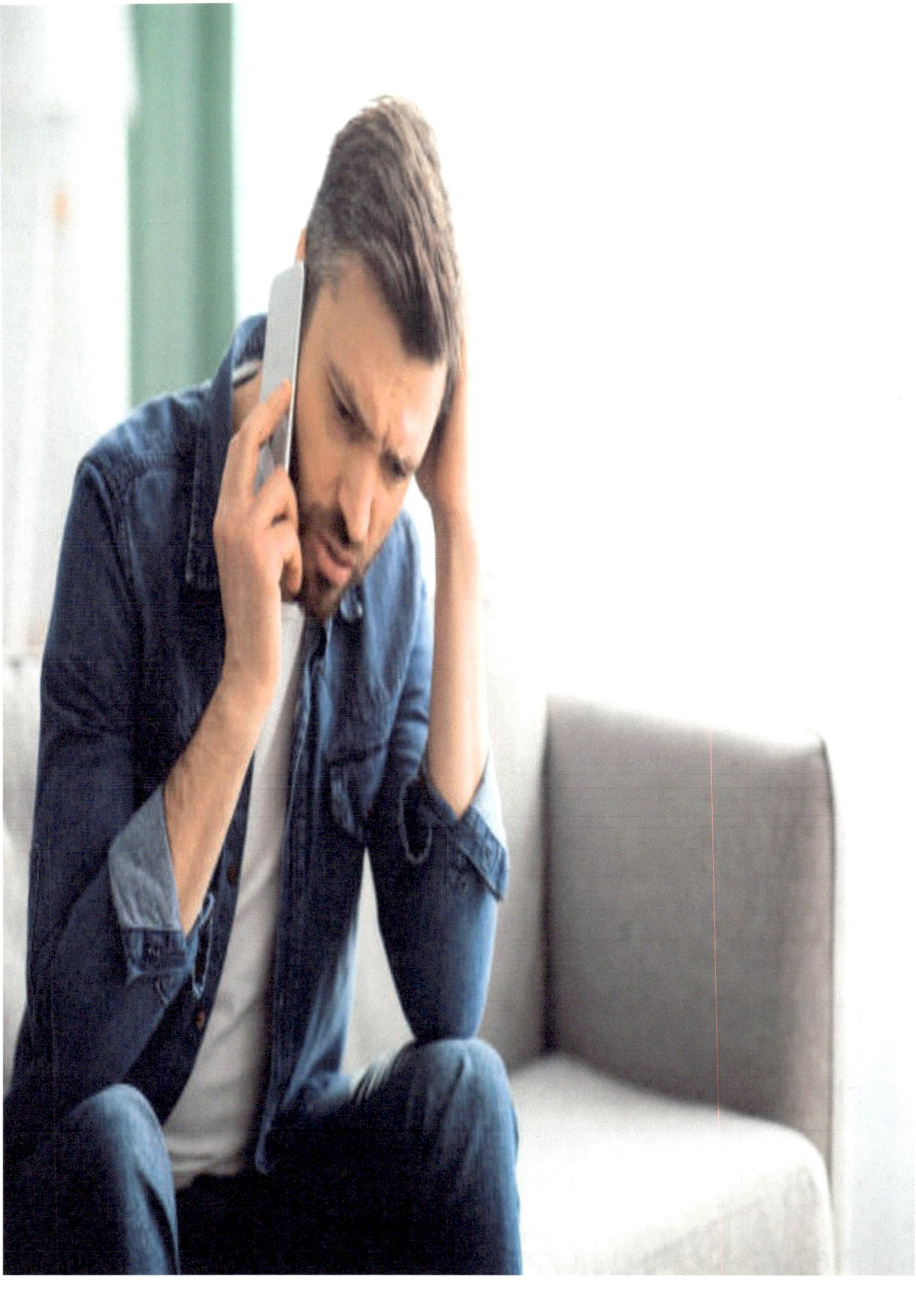

Phone lines buzzed with discussions about Reverend Brown motives, the amount of money involved, and the potential consequences for the church. Some members expressed outrage and disappointment, feeling betrayed by their trusted leader.

Others were more measured in their responses, choosing to reserve judgment until more information became available. As the gossip mill continued to churn, some church members began to feel uncomfortable. They worried that the focus on the scandal and speculation was distracting from the church's mission and values.

They encouraged their fellow members to focus on prayer, healing, and rebuilding, rather than getting caught up in rumors and gossip. The church leadership, too, recognized the need to address gossip and speculation. They issued a statement urging members to refrain from spreading rumors and to focus on supporting one another during this challenging time.

As the church navigated this challenging period, they were reminded of the importance of maintaining a spirit of love, compassion, and forgiveness – even in the face of adversity. That is a common reaction in many communities. Here are some thoughts:

The news of Reverend Brown's embezzlement sent shockwaves through the church community.

As the reality of the situation sank in, church members began to reach out to each other, sharing their thoughts, feelings, and reactions. While some conversations were supportive and focused on praying for the church and its leaders, others quickly turned to gossip and speculation.

As the gossip mill continued to churn, some church members began to feel uncomfortable. They worried that the focus on scandal and speculation was distracting from the church's mission and values. They encouraged their fellow members to focus on prayer, healing, and rebuilding, rather than getting caught up in rumors and gossip. The church leadership, too, recognized the need to address gossip and speculation. They issued a statement urging members to refrain from spreading rumors and to focus on supporting one another during this grim time.

As the church navigated this challenging period, they were reminded of the importance of maintaining a

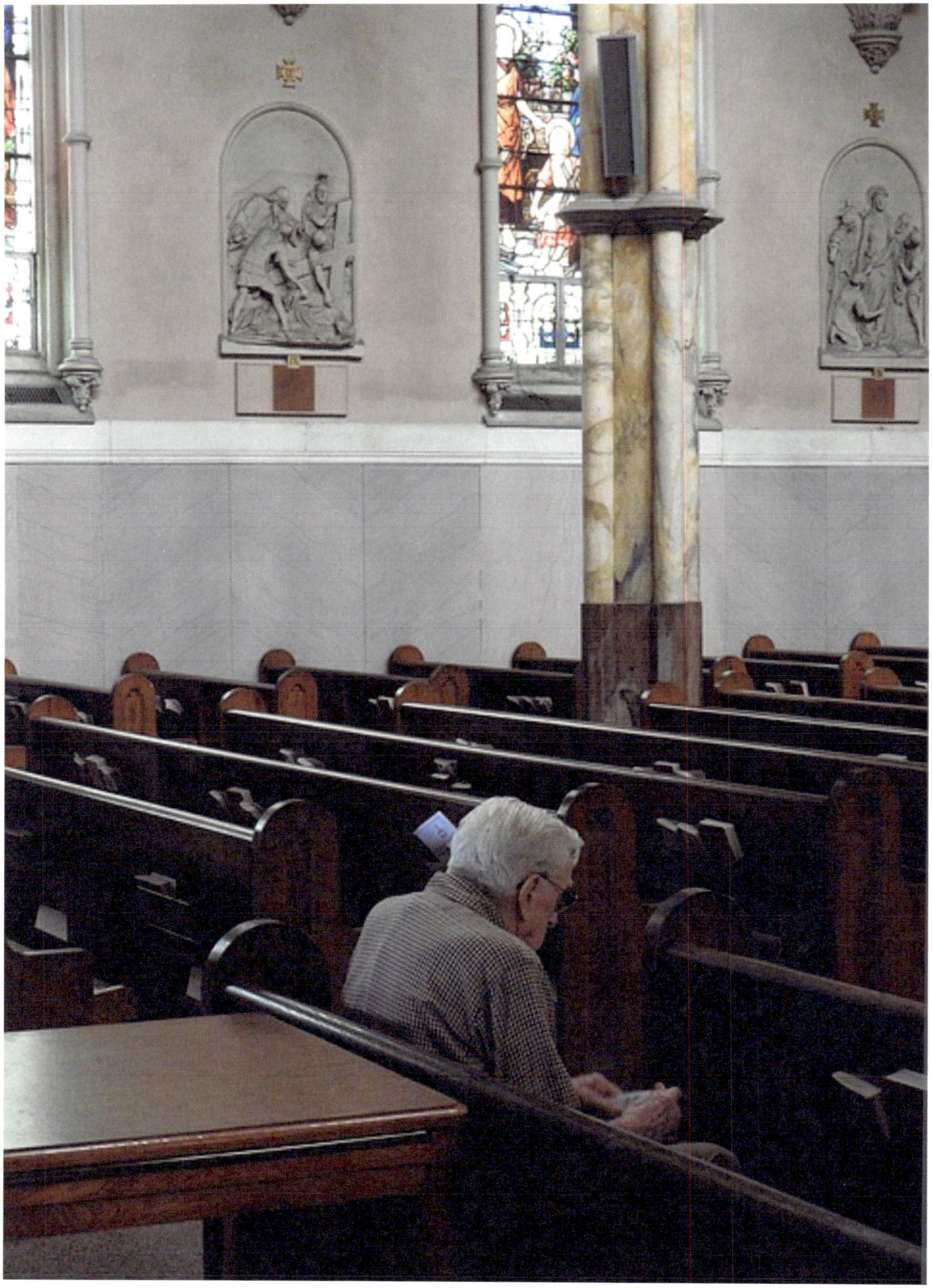

spirit of love, compassion, and forgiveness – even in the face of adversity.

An astronomical decline in the church's attendance took place. As the news spread more, and more, Visitors did not show up. Some of the most faithful members stopped attending altogether. Others came to express their outrage and demand answers.

The scandal eroded the trust between the church leadership and its members.

It would take time, effort, and transparency to rebuild that trust in the community.

The Church Board produced many helpful initiatives to regain community trust. The initiatives are as follows:

1. Host a free potluck dinner where members can share food and fellowship, fostering a sense of community and connection.

2. Organize free beach parties, providing a fun and relaxed atmosphere for members to bond and create memories.

3. Host a black-tie (or black and white-themed) banquet at the church, inviting the community to come together and celebrate.

4. Plan regular family fun days with activities, games, and entertainment, providing a safe and enjoyable environment for families to spend time together.

5. Organize community service projects, such as food drives, charity events, or volunteer days, to

demonstrate the church's commitment to serving the community.

6. Continue to prioritize transparency and accountability, providing regular updates on the church's finances and governance.

7. Recognize and celebrate members' contributions, milestones, and achievements, fostering a sense of appreciation and belonging.

8 Ensure that pastoral care and support are available to members, providing a safe and confidential space to share concerns and receive guidance.

By implementing these initiatives, the church can take steps towards rebuilding trust, fostering a sense of community, and promoting a positive, inclusive environment for all members.

Chapter 7

Financial Consequences

The church faced financial repercussions, including potential lawsuits and reimbursement demands from donors who had been deceived.

As the news of Reverend Brown's embezzlement spread, many church members felt betrayed and hurt. Some of them decided to take legal action, filing lawsuits against the church and Reverend Brown. However, as they reflected on their decision, they began to wonder if taking legal action was truly in line with their Christian values.

.They remembered the words of Jesus, who taught them to forgive and love their enemies. One member, in particular, felt convicted by the scripture in Matthew 18:21-22, where Jesus says, "Then Peter came to Jesus and asked, 'Lord, how many times shall I forgive my brother or sister who sins against me? Up to seven times?' Jesus answered, 'I tell you, not seven times, but seventy-seven times.'

Another member of the church shared these scriptures. "Here are some scriptures that emphasize the importance of forgiveness as God's people:"

1. Matthew 6:14-15- "For if you forgive other people when they sin against you, your heavenly Father will also forgive you. But if you do not forgive others their sins, your Father will not forgive your sins." 2. Mark 11:25 - "And when you stand praying, if you hold

anything against anyone, forgive them, so that your Father in heaven may forgive you your sins." 3. Luke 6:37-38 - "Do not judge, and you will not be judged. Do not condemn, and you will not be condemned. Forgive, and you will be forgiven. Give, and it will be given to you." 4. Colossians 3:13 - "Bear with each other and forgive one another if any of you have a grievance against someone. Forgive as the Lord forgave you." 5. *Ephesians 4:32* - "Be kind and compassionate to one another, forgiving each other, just as in Christ God forgave you." These scriptures remind us that forgiveness is a fundamental aspect of our relationship with God and with others. By choosing to forgive, we reflect God's character and demonstrate our trust in His sovereignty.

As they pondered these words, the church members began to see that taking legal action might not be the

best course of action. They realized that forgiveness and restoration were more in line with Jesus' teachings. After much prayer and reflection, each of The church members decided to drop their lawsuits against the church. They claimed that the council leaders were truly blind sited into Rev. Brown's actions.

Instead, they chose to focus on healing, restoration, and rebuilding their community.

This decision was not easy, but it was a testament to their commitment to living out their Christian faith. By choosing to forgive and extend mercy, they demonstrated that they valued their relationship with

God and with each other more than material possessions or revenge.

As they moved forward, the church members continued to grapple with the aftermath of the embezzlement. However, they did so with a renewed sense of purpose and commitment to living out their faith in a way that honored God.

They all agreed that the God they served, "Give the toughest battles to the strongest solders

Chapter 8

Arrested

The confrontation continues to set off longer chain reaction of events that exposes Reverend Brown's deceit to the entire community. The church was thrown into turmoil, and Reverend Brown's reputation was left in tatters.

The Church Board wanted to drop all the allegations and refrain from involving law enforcements. However, every negative action has its consequences. Law Enforcement is in place for such a time as this. "Crime has its consequences."

After conducting a thorough investigation, the church council decided to press charges against Reverend Brown for embezzlement and fraud. They worked closely with local law enforcement to gather evidence and build a persuasive case. Evidence of Excess As the investigation into Rev. Brown's finances continued, a trail of evidence emerged that painted a picture of extravagance and excess. Among the findings were: First-class plane tickets to exotic destinations around the world - Monthly massages at high-end spas - Luxury cruises to the Caribbean and Mediterranean - Frequent trips to third-world countries, where the exchange rate allowed him to live like royalty on a modest budget It was discovered that Rev. Brown had been taking advantage of the favorable exchange rates in countries like Argentina, Brazil, and South Africa. With $200 USD yielding as much as $4,084.80 in some of these countries.

Rev. Brown was able to indulge in luxuries that would have been unaffordable in the United States.

The evidence of Rev. Brown's lavish spending habits raised fundamental questions about his stewardship of church funds and his commitment to serving the needs of his congregation. As the scandal continued to unfold, Rev. Brown's reputation and legacy continues to crumble.

Reverend Brown was arrested and charged with multiple counts of embezzlement and fraud. He faced dire consequences, including fines, restitution, and potentially even jail time.

Chapter 9

Healing and Restoration

Eventually, the church began the process of healing and restoration. This involved appointing new leadership, implementing stricter financial controls, and providing counseling and support to affected members.

The church appointed a new pastor, who brought a fresh perspective and a commitment to transparency and accountability.

The church refocused on its core mission and values, emphasizing the importance of integrity, honesty, and compassion. Over time, the church was able to rebuild trust with its members and the wider community, emerging stronger and more resilient than before.

THIS NOTE IS LEGAL TENDER
FOR ALL DEBTS, PUBLIC AND PRIVATE
Treasurer of the United States
FEDERAL RESERVE
HC 38553
C3
G7
100

The church also took steps to recover the stolen funds and to prevent similar incidents in the future.

They implemented new financial controls, increased transparency, and provided training for churches. leaders on ethics and accountability.

No single person, including the pastor, had control over all financial transactions.

Responsibilities were divided among multiple individuals.

 All checks and financial transactions required two signatures, ensuring that at least two people reviewed and approved of each transaction. The church hired an independent auditor to review their financial statements annually, providing an objective assessment of their monetary management.

Regular financial reports were provided to the church council and congregation, promoting transparency and accountability.

A detailed budget was created, and expenses were closely tracked to prevent unauthorized spending.

The church implemented electronic payment systems for donations and expenses, reducing the handling of cash and increasing security.

Background checks were conducted on all church staff and volunteers managing finances.

A comprehensive financial policy manual was created, outlining procedures for monetary management, accounting, and reporting

Chapter 10

The conviction:

Rev. Brown stood before the judge and jury, his eyes cast downward in a mixture of shame and defiance. Despite the overwhelming evidence against him, he still pleaded not guilty to the charges of embezzling funds from the church offerings.

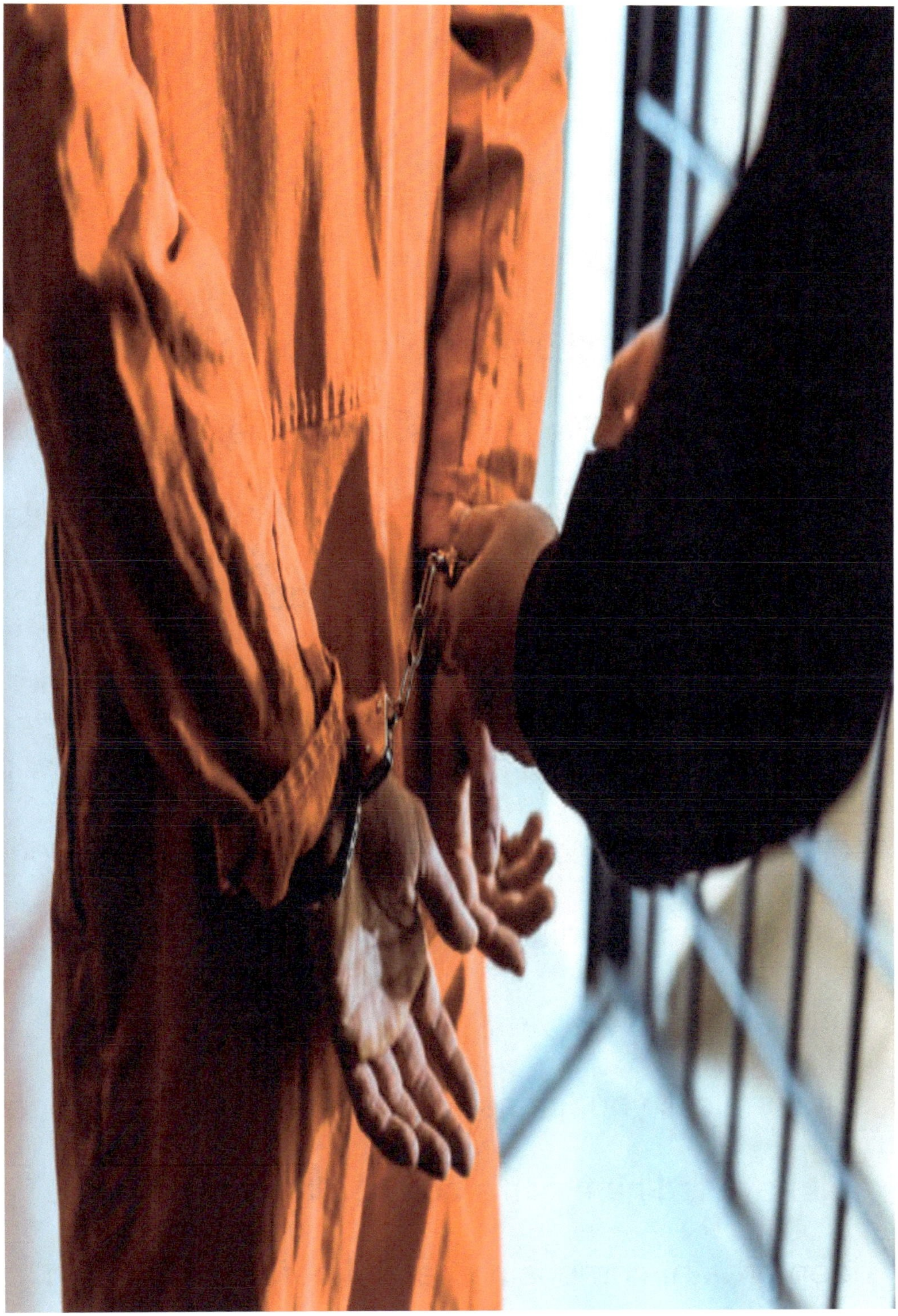

Rev. Brown's mother, Mrs. Brown, stood before the judge, her eyes filled with tears and her voice trembling with emotion. She had always been a pillar of strength for her son, and now she was determined to advocate for him in his time of need. "Your Honor," she began, her voice cracking with sorrow. "I know my son, Rev. Brown, has made mistakes. He has failed in his duties as a minister, and for that, he is terribly sorry.

But I implore you, please consider the circumstances that have led him to this point." Mrs. Brown took a deep breath, composing herself before continuing. "Rev. Brown grew up without a father. His father abandoned our family when He was just a two-year-old child, leaving us to struggle to make ends meet. The elderly woman's voice continued to trembly as she spoke, her eyes filled with a deep sense of sorrow and regret. "To the church community, again, I offer my sincerest apologies for the pain and hurt my son has caused. I understand that his actions have brought shame and disappointment to our community, and for that, I am truly sorry." She paused, collecting her thoughts before continuing. "While I have no control over my son's behavior, I am aware that some of his actions stem from his upbringing. As a single mother, I did the best I could to raise him, but I know that I couldn't provide the guidance and discipline that a father figure could." Her voice cracked as she spoke, the weight of her words evident. "A mother cannot raise men; men raise men.

And in my son's life, that presence was sadly lacking. His father was not around, and I was left to navigate the challenges of parenting alone." The room fell silent, the only sound the soft sniffles of those moved by her words. "So, I beg of you, please forgive my son. Forgive him for the pain he has caused. Forgive me for not being able to provide him with the upbringing he deserved. I pray that you will be able to find it in your hearts to forgive and that we can work together to heal and move forward."

My son suffered from childhood trauma, and mental health issues. He struggled with anxiety, depression, and feelings of abandonment. The judge looked up from the papers on his desk, his expression softening slightly as he listened to Mrs. Brown's words. Despite these challenges, Rev. Brown grew into a kind, compassionate, and resolute individual. Mrs. Brown continued. He became a minister, not just as a profession, but as a calling. He genuinely wanted to help others, to be effective in their lives. Mrs. Brown's voice broke again, and she paused, collecting herself before speaking again. But, Your Honor, my son's past, has continued to haunt him. See, here are some psychological documentations to prove that he has been evaluated with some issues.

The childhood trauma and mental health issues have lingered, affecting his judgment and decision-making. I am not making excuses for his actions, but I am asking you to consider the context in which they occurred

I am not surprised to have learned he has been sending money to foreign countries to feed the hungry children. I promise you; He has placed himself in those children's condition. Psychology, he is still experiencing the lack that the children are facing.

I'm not asking for leniency because my son is a minister," Mrs. Brown concluded. "I'm asking because he is a human being flawed and imperfect, just like the rest of us. He deserves compassion, understanding, and a second chance."

As Mrs. Brown finished speaking, the judge looked at Rev. Brown, who was seated in the defendant's chair, his head bowed in shame. The judge's expression was inscrutable, but Mrs. Brown held onto hope, praying that her words had had an influence.

A community member, Mrs. Godet, sat in the court room with her eyes fixed on the judge as she waited for her chance to speak. She had written a letter to the judge, telling him about the impact Rev. Brown had had on her life.

As she stood before the judge, her voice trembled with emotion. "Your Honor, I'm here today to speak on behalf of Rev. Brown. I know he's made mistakes, but I also know that he's a good man who has helped many people in our community." She took a deep breath, collecting her thoughts before continuing. "Rev. Brown saved my life, Your Honor. He stopped me from committing suicide when I was at my lowest point. He prayed with me, counseled me, and helped me to see that there was still hope." Mrs. Godet's eyes filled with tears as she remembered the dark days she had faced. "Rev. Brown was there for me when I needed him most. He showed me kindness, compassion, and love. And I know he's done the same for many others." She looked directly at the judge, her voice filled with conviction. "I'm not asking you to let Rev. Brown off scot-free, Your Honor. But I am asking you to consider the good he's done, and to show him mercy." The judge looked at Mrs. Godet, with thoughtful expressions. He nodded, taking her words into consideration.

"Your Honor, the defense would like to present a crucial piece of information that sheds light on Rev. Brown's troubled past. It is a painful and disturbing truth, but one that is essential to understanding the complexities of Rev. Brown's character. Rev. Brown suffered from Fetal Alcohol Syndrome, a condition caused by his mother's exposure to severe physical and emotional trauma during her pregnancy. The court has obtained records and testimony confirming that Rev. Brown's pregnant mother was brutally beaten and kicked repeatedly, subjected to unimaginable cruelty and disregard for human life. This traumatic event had a profound impact on Rev. Brown's fetal development, affecting his brain function, emotional regulation, and behavioral patterns.

The trauma inflicted upon his mother was in effect, inflicted upon him, leaving an indelible mark on his psyche."

Children whose mothers were beaten while pregnant may experience various effects, which can be influenced by several factors: Let us examine some crucial facts checks:

**Physical Effects:**

1. **Low Birth Weight:** Trauma during pregnancy can lead to premature birth or low birth weight.

2. **Fetal Distress:** Physical abuse can cause fetal distress, which may result in birth complications.

3. **Developmental Delays:** Prenatal exposure to violence may affect fetal brain development, leading to delays in cognitive, emotional, and physical development.

**Emotional and Psychological Effects:**

1. **Anxiety and Stress:** Children may experience increased anxiety and stress due to the traumatic prenatal environment.

2. **Emotional Regulation**: Difficulty regulating emotions, leading to mood swings, irritability, or explosive behavior.

3. **Attachment Issues:** Children may struggle with forming healthy attachments to caregivers due to the traumatic prenatal experience.

4. **Increased Risk of PTSD:** Children may be more susceptible to developing post-traumatic stress disorder (PTSD) later in life.

**Behavioral Effects:**

1. **Aggression:** Children may exhibit aggressive behavior, such as fighting or tantrums.

2. **Hyperactivity**: Prenatal exposure to violence may contribute to attention deficit hyperactivity disorder (ADHD) symptoms.

3. **Social Withdrawal:** Children may become withdrawn or isolated, struggling to form healthy relationships with peers.

**Long-term Effects**

1. **Intergenerational Trauma:**

Children may be more likely to experience or perpetuate violence in their own relationships.

2. **Mental Health Concerns**: Increased risk of developing mental health conditions, such as depression, anxiety disorders, or personality disorders.

3. **Substance Abuse** : Children may be more vulnerable to substance abuse or addiction.

It is essential to recognize that each child's response to prenatal trauma can vary, and some may not exhibit any noticeable effects. Providing a nurturing environment, counseling, and support can help mitigate the potential effects of prenatal trauma. Lifetime of struggles and poor decision-making.

The defense is not attempting to excuse Rev. Brown's actions, but rather to provide context and understanding. The facts are clear. Why did Rev. Brown display such heinous behavior?

We urge the court to consider the mitigating factors that contributed to Rev. Brown's behavior, and to weigh these factors in determining an appropriate sentence.

The prosecutor presented some strong evidence. Affidavits revealing a trail of financial records and eyewitness testimony that implicated Rev. Brown in the theft.

The prosecutor's voice was filled with emotion as he presented his case against Rev. Brown. He painted a vivid picture of the many lives that had been impacted by the reverend's actions. "Your Honor, the defendant, Rev. Brown, has been entrusted with the care and spiritual guidance of this community. He has been a figure of trust, respect, and admiration for many. However, his actions have shattered that trust and broken the hearts of those who looked up to him." The prosecutor paused, surveying the courtroom before continuing. "We have senior citizens who entrusted their life savings to Rev. Brown, believing that he would use it for the betterment of the community. We have children who saw him as a father figure, who confided in him, and who sought his guidance. We have single parents who worked tirelessly, often holding down two jobs, just to put a little extra money in the offering plate, believing that it would be used for the glory of God." The prosecutor's voice cracked with emotion as he spoke "And then there are the children, innocent and pure of heart, who emptied their piggy banks into the offering plate, believing that they were contributing to something greater than themselves. Rev. Brown, you broke their hearts. You shattered their trust. You took advantage of their innocence." The prosecutor's words hung in the air, a stark reminder of the devastating impact of Rev. Brown's actions. The courtroom was silent, the only sound the quiet sobbing of those who had been hurt by the reverend's betrayal.

The church members who had trusted him with their tithes and offerings felt betrayed and hurt by his actions.

As the jury deliberated, Rev. Brown's fate hung in the balance.

The Jurors felt pressured to reach a verdict. They thoroughly examine the evidence, weighing its credibility and reliability. They work hard to be certain that Justice is served, and the rights of all parties are protected. After many hours, they finally return with a guilty verdict.

After a moment of silence, the judge spoke. "Rev. Brown, I've taken into account the many testimonies about your good work in the community. I've also considered Mrs. Godet's heartfelt plea on your behalf." Rev. Brown looked up; his eyes filled with hope. The judge continued. "While you have made mistakes, I believe that you have the potential to make a positive impact on your community.

I have decided to grant you a reduced sentence of one year in prison. I am ordering you to pay restitution to the church and to undergo counseling to address your mishaps.

You see, these are the statics for the nature of your crime; given the circumstances; The number of years for embezzlement can vary greatly. It is based on the severity of the offense, and the specific circumstances of the case. These are the Sentencing Ranges:

Misdemeanor embezzlement: 1-3 years

Felony embezzlement: 2-10 years

Aggravated embezzlement (e.g., large sums of money, repeat offenses): 5-20 years.

Factors Affecting Sentencing: Amount of money embezzled.

Duration of the embezzlement scheme,

Position of trust or authority held by the offender,

Number of victims affected,

Level of sophistication or planning involved.

Offender's prior record and criminal history

Examples of Embezzlement Sentences - A former employee who embezzled $10,000 from their company might receive a sentence of 2-5 years.

A CEO who embezzled $1 million from their company might receive a sentence of 10-20 years. A public official who embezzled $500,000 from government funds might receive a sentence of 5-15 years.

Keep in mind that these are general estimates, and actual sentencing can vary significantly. Your mishaps had a long ongoing timeline. You are getting a slap on the risk.

So, appreciate the people who spoke on your behalf here today. Their care, concern, and love have really helped to shape your sentencing. God bless you, Rev. Brown.

As Rev. Brown was led away in handcuffs, his mother screamed, "Please pray for my son.

The church members who had once looked up to him as a spiritual leader felt a sense of sadness and loss.

They had trusted him, and he had abused that trust.

The incident served as a painful reminder that even those in positions of authority can fall prey to temptation and greed. The church would have to heal from the betrayal.

For Rev. Brown, the consequences of his actions would be severe and long-lasting. The memories of him taking advantage of his church's community will have a lasting impact on all who have been under his leadership.

Chapter 11

Fallen From Grace

Reverend Brown's fall from grace was swift and merciless. He went from being a respected community leader to a convicted felon, sentenced to two years in prison.

As he navigated the harsh realities of prison life, Reverend Brown encountered a man named Delmas. Delmas was a gruff nonsense individual who had spent years behind bars. Despite his tough exterior, Delmas had a soft spot for those in need and took Reverend Brown under his wing. Delmas was a devout Christian who had found faith during his time in prison. He saw something in Reverend Brown that no one else did. Delmas saw some potential for redemption.

Delmas took it upon himself to mentor Reverend Brown, teaching him about the true meaning of faith, forgiveness, and second chances. Rev. Brown confided his downfall in Delmas.

As Reverend Brown sat in his prison cell, surrounded by the cold, unforgiving walls, he felt the weight of his sins crushing him. He thought about the people he had hurt, the trust he had betrayed, and the shame he had brought upon himself and his family. In a moment of raw desperation, Reverend Brown cried out to God, his voice shaking with emotion: "Oh, God, forgive me! I have sinned against you and against those who trusted me. I have been blinded by my own pride and greed. I am ashamed of what I have done." As he prayed, Reverend Brown felt a sense of humility wash over him. He realized that he had been living a lie, using his position of power to feed his own ego and desires. "Lord, I repent of my sins," Reverend Brown continued, his voice cracking with emotion. "I ask for your forgiveness and your mercy. Help me to make amends for the harm I have caused and to start anew." In that moment, Reverend Brown felt a sense of peace settle over him. He knew that he still had a long way to go, but he also knew that he was on the path to redemption.

Brown sat in his prison cell, his hands trembling as he held the pen. He had been incarcerated for weeks now, convicted of crimes that had shaken his community to its core. As he began to write, Rev. Brown's thoughts turned to his wife, Sarah. He had hurt her deeply, and he knew that he had lost her trust. But he hoped that she would find it in her heart to forgive him.

"My dearest Sarah, I write to you today with a heart full of sorrow and regret. I am deeply ashamed of my actions, and I can only imagine the pain and hurt that I have caused you. As I sit in this cell, I am forced to confront the darkness that has been within me for so long. I have been a hypocrite, preaching one thing while living another. I have brought shame to our family, our church, and our community. But even amid this darkness, I have found a glimmer of hope. I have come to realize that I am not beyond redemption, that I can still seek forgiveness and work towards healing. Sarah, I know that I do not deserve your forgiveness. But I hope that you will find it in your heart to pardon me. I promise to spend the rest of my days making amends, seeking counseling, and working to rebuild the trust that I have broken. If you are willing, I would like to begin the process of healing and restoration. I want to work towards rebuilding our marriage, and I am willing to do whatever it takes to regain your trust. Hoping one day to become the trusted leader you once knew.

As Rev. Brown finished writing the letter, he felt a sense of hope that he had not felt in months. He knew that the road ahead would be long and difficult, but he was determined to make things right. And so, he prayed:

Dear Heavenly Father, I, Rev. Brown, come before you with a humble and contrite heart. I acknowledge my sins and confess them before you. Lord, I have failed you and fallen short of your glory. My actions have not reflected the righteousness and holiness that you demand from your servants. I repent of my sins, Lord. I turn away from the wickedness that has consumed me, and I turn towards you, seeking your forgiveness and mercy. Wash me clean, Lord, and make me whole again. Restore me to a right relationship with you and renew my spirit that I may serve you with integrity, honesty, and humility. Thank you, Lord, for your love and forgiveness. Thank you for the gift of salvation and for the promise of eternal life. In Jesus' name, I pray. Amen.

# SUMMARY

The Preacher's Deceit is a gripping drama that explores the darker side of human nature. Thus, his action stems from his embryo stress.

Through its thought-provoking storyline and complex characters, this book raises important questions about morality, trust, and the corrupting influence of power. Reverend Brown was a well-respected pastor in his community. A true man of God, Holy Ghost F known for his charismatic sermons and compassionate demeanor. However, beneath his pious exterior lay a corrupt and dishonest individual.

 As the church's financial leader, Reverend Brown had access to its vast funds and resources. Over time, he began to abuse this trust, using the church's money to finance his own lavish lifestyle. His eyes were always scanning for opportunities to embezzle funds, and his hands were quick to grab whatever he could. He would often use church money to buy expensive cars, jewelry, and luxury vacations.

Despite his corrupt ways, Reverend Brown maintained a facade of integrity. He would preach honesty and morality, while secretly living a life of deceit and greed. The church's members were oblivious to Reverend Brown's embezzlement, and they continued to trust him with their donations. But as time went on, the Reverend's corruption only deepened.

As he sat in his jail cell, he realized that he had excluded himself from the very commandments he had preached. He had stolen from the church, lied to his congregation.

Rev. Brown's downfall was a cautionary tale about the dangers of hypocrisy and the importance of living by the principles we preach.

In the end, Reverend Brown was brought to justice, and the church began the process of healing and rebuilding.

References:

New International Version
Wikipedia
 https://en.wikipedia.org › wiki › New_International_

The New International Version (NIV) is a translation of the Bible into contemporary English. Published by Biblica,


My Perspective on Abusive Behaviors: Lynette Allana Hopson
2019 ISBN: 9-798 722 4865 7-8


Wikipedia
https:// in. Wikipedia.org….wiki Embezzlement
Embezzlement

Embezzlement is a term commonly used for a type of financial crime, usually involving theft of money from a business or employer.
Larceny

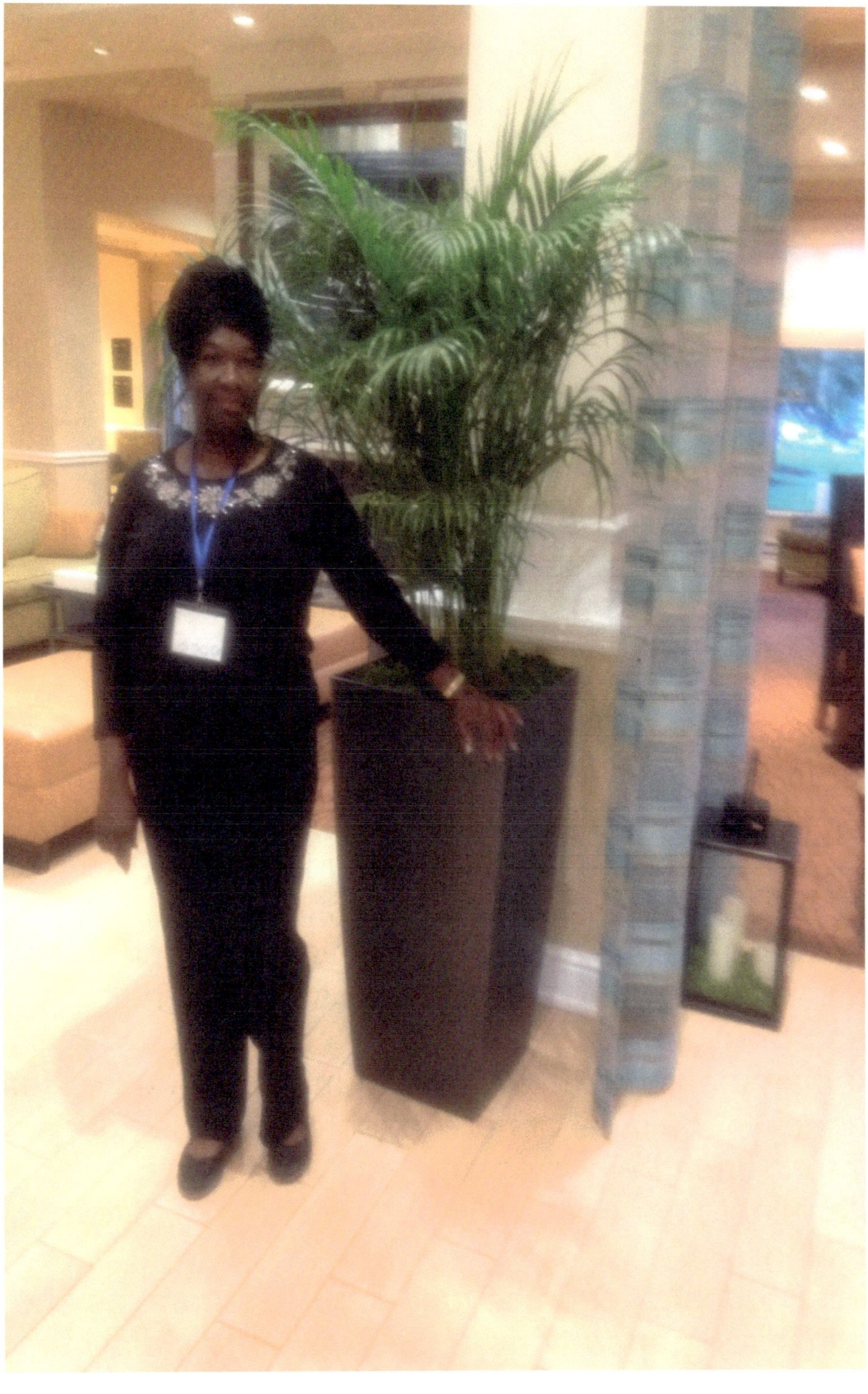

## About the Author

Lynette (Wilma) is a renowned educator with a remarkable 40-year teaching career, has left an indelible mark on the lives of countless students across various institutions.

Her dedication, passion, and commitment to education have earned her a reputation as an exceptional teacher and mentor.

Throughout her illustrious career, Wilma has had the privilege of teaching at several esteemed institutions, including:

1. Good Shepherd School in the US Virgin Islands, where she began her teaching journey, instilling values, and knowledge in young minds.
2. Norfolk Public Schools in Virginia, where she continued to nurture and educate students, helping shape their futures.
3. Indianapolis Public Schools in Indiana, she has left a legacy in the lives of her students and colleagues.

Her four-decade-long commitment to education is a testament to her perseverance, patience, and love for teaching.

Her influence extends beyond the classroom, as she has inspired generations of students, many of whom have gone on to become successful individuals in their respective fields.

As a resolute educator, She has demonstrated exceptional skills in: Classroom management and instruction Curriculum development and implementation Student assessment and evaluation Parent-teacher communication and collaboration Community engagement and outreach Throughout her career Wilma has been recognized for her outstanding contributions to education, receiving accolades and awards for her tireless efforts.

Her legacy serves as a shining example for aspiring educators, reminding them of the transformative power of teaching and the impact one resolute individual can have on the lives of countless students.

John 3:16: For God so love the World that he giveth His only Son…

Isaiah 43:19: Behold I the Lord will make a river in the wilderness…

CONTRIBUTIONS :   2024----2025

Wilma Gittens

James Compton :

Michael Cornelious:

Orianna Kaha:

Brian Parker:

Made in United States
Troutdale, OR
03/13/2025